THE SEVEN DWARFS

AN EROTIC FAIRYTALE

CLOVER'S FANTASY ADVENTURES
BOOK 9

VICTORIA RUSH

VOLUME 9

CLOVER'S FANTASY ADVENTURES -
BOOK 9

COPYRIGHT

The Seven Dwarfs © 2023 Victoria Rush

Cover Design © 2023 PhotoMaras

ALSO BY VICTORIA RUSH

Adult Fairytales:

The Enchanted Forest: An Erotic Fairytale

The Land of Giants: An Erotic Fairytale

The Dragon's Lair: An Erotic Fairytale

Witch's Brew: An Erotic Fairytale

The Mage's Spell: An Erotic Fairytale

The Mermaid Lagoon: An Erotic Fairytale

The Coven: An Erotic Fairytale

Rapunzel: An Erotic Fairytale

The Seven Dwarfs: An Erotic Fairytale

The Land of Mutants: An Erotic Fairytale

The Erotic Temple: A Sexy Fairytale (Coming Soon)

Erotica Themed Bundles:

Voyeur: Lesbian Erotica Bundle

Public Affairs: A Lesbian Anthology

Futa Fantasies: The Ladyboy Collection

Threesomes: The Lesbian Collection

Threesomes - Volume 2: The Lesbian Collection

First Time: A Lesbian Anthology

Hedonism: An Erotic Anthology

Switch Hitters: Bisexual Erotica

Taboo Erotica: The Lesbian Series

BDSM: The Lesbian Collection

Party Games: The Erotic Collection

Party Games 2: The Erotic Collection

All Girl 1: Lesbian Erotica Bundle

All Girl 2: Lesbian Erotica Bundle

All Girl 3: Lesbian Erotica Bundle

All Girl 4: Lesbian Erotica Bundle

Erotic Fairytale Bundles:

Clover's Fantasy Adventures: Books 1 - 5

Clover's Fantasy Adventures: Books 6 - 10

Erotic Fantasy:

Pirate's Bounty: A Time Travel Adventure

Wild West: A Time Travel Adventure

Private Riley: A Time Travel Adventure

Cleopatra's Secret: A Time Travel Adventure

Bounty Hunter 2125: A Time Travel Adventure

Ninja Assassin: A Time Travel Adventure

The 300: A Time Travel Adventure

Arabian Nights: An Erotic Fairytale (coming soon...)

Steamy Time Travel Bundles:

Riley's Time Travel Adventures: Books 1 - 5

Lesbian Erotica:

Tribadism 1: Girls Only Sex Workshop

Tribadism 2: The Art of Scissoring

Tribadism 3: Threeway Hookups

The Kiss: A Game of Oral Sex

Pledge Week: Sorority Sisters

Carny Games 1: A Wild Sex Party

Carny Games 2: A Kinky Sex Party

Carny Games 3: An Erotic Sex Party

Dreamscape: An Artificial Reality Game

Glory Hole: Guess Who's On the Other Side

Joy Ride: A Late Night Erotic Bus Trip

The Blind Girl: An Erotic Romance(Coming Soon)

Lesbian Erotica Bundles:

Jade's Erotic Adventures: Books 1 - 5

Jade's Erotic Adventures: Books 6 - 10

Jade's Erotic Adventures: Books 11 - 15

Jade's Erotic Adventures: Books 16 - 20

Jade's Erotic Adventures: Books 21 - 25

Jade's Erotic Adventures: Books 26 - 30

Standalone Stories:

The Polynesian Girl: A Lesbian EroticRomance

For the uninhibited...

WANT TO AMP UP YOUR SEX LIFE?

Sign up for my newsletter to receive more free books and other steamy stuff. Discover a hundred different ways to wet your whistle!

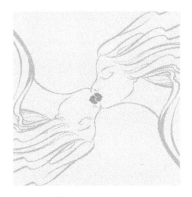

Victoria Rush Erotica

1

After Rapunzel and her friends parted ways, Clover, Tara, and Jessop decided to head inland to forage for food. A couple of hours later, they stumbled upon a remote cottage in the woods, and Tara lifted her hand, signaling for the group to take cover while they scoped the place out. There was an odd-looking man working in a large vegetable garden, and they peered at him through squinted eyes, deciding if it was safe to approach.

"He looks harmless enough," Clover said, glancing at his short britches held up by criss-crossing suspenders. "I think he's some kind of dwarf."

"There doesn't appear to be anyone else in the house," Jessop nodded, peering up at the idle chimney.

"But that's a pretty big garden for one person," Tara said, darting her eyes suspiciously over the surrounding property. "We better approach carefully in case he has friends in the area."

"Maybe we can ask him for some fresh vegetables?" Clover said, hiking up the string of dead rabbits slung over her shoulder. "It would be nice to have some garnishes to go with our wild game for dinner tonight."

"Especially if he's growing the food for sale," Jessop nodded.

"Okay," Tara said, watching Jessop holding his hand over the hilt of his sword as he slowly approached the man. "But keep your weapons concealed so as not to scare him."

As the trio approached the man from three sides, he noticed movement out of the corner of his eye and reared up, raising his rake over his head defensively.

"Who goes there?" he said, waving the tool in front of his quivering chest.

"We mean no harm," Clover said, raising her palms. "We were wondering if you might have some surplus rations that you could share with some hungry travelers. We'd be happy to pay you for anything you can share."

The man paused as he appraised the group, scanning Clover's and Tara's tight-fitting bodysuits, then he slowly lowered his rake.

"Are you from the *village*?" he said.

"No," Tara said. "We've been traveling for some distance and are just stopping to pick up some provisions."

The dwarf turned toward Jessop and examined his athletic build, peering at his sword resting by his side.

"You're a bit of an odd combination for traveling vagabonds," he said. "Two women and a man, traveling alone. Are you related?"

"We could say the same of *you*," Clover said. "A strange man tending crops all by himself in the middle of the forest..."

"I don't live here alone," he said, motioning to the front of his cottage where a group of similar sized dwarfs tilted the door open, peering at the three friends with bemused interest. "If you're hungry, you're welcome to come inside and share a meal with my friends. It looks like you've got enough meat to feed all of us."

Clover paused as she inspected the group of gnomes bunched up around the entrance. They didn't appear to be carrying any weapons, and in their funny costumes they looked like something more out of a children's fairy tale than a threatening menace. But there was something about the unusual pouches on the front of their pants that seemed out of place. Instead of the usual zipper or button closure, the loose and bulging flaps appeared to be held up by a simple hook and grommet. She turned toward her friends and shrugged her shoulders, signaling that it seemed safe to proceed.

"Okay," Tara said, looking toward Jessop, who nodded in agreement. "We'll be happy to share our bounty if you'll add some greens from your garden."

"Of course," the man said, motioning for his friends to allow them into the house. "We're always happy to share our spoils with famished travelers."

The group followed the man into his cottage, then he turned around to introduce himself.

"My name's Randy," he said. "And these are my friends, Frisky, Itchy, Noisy, Kinky, Splashy, and Jumbo."

Clover couldn't help snickering at the funny names of the dwarves.

"Those are some pretty interesting names," she chuckled, motioning toward her friends. "My name's Clover, and these are my friends Tara and Jessop."

"Help yourself to a seat at our table," Randy said, pointing toward a large, oblong bench while the other gnomes scurried to fetch some extra chairs. "Rest your legs while our band cooks up some rabbit stew."

The three friends sat together at one end of the table as the dwarves bustled around their makeshift kitchen, chopping the meat while the others sliced an assortment of vegetables, dropping them into a steaming pot on the stove. The cottage had one small central room comprising the kitchen on one side and some upholstered furniture on the other next to the fireplace, with an elevated dormitory surrounding the perimeter of the room, accessible by a single wooden ladder. There wasn't much decoration in the place, save a strange-looking mold of a woman's ass resting on stilts next to the fireplace.

She peered at her friends with a wrinkled forehead, tilting her head toward the strange-looking object, wondering what they'd gotten themselves into with this odd assortment of weird-looking men. But within a short period of time, the dwarves had cooked up a delicious-smelling stew, placing steaming bowls of broth on their place settings and joining them at the table. Randy poured some wine from a decanter into each of their goblets, then he raised his cup in honor of his guests.

"To our wandering guests," he said, nodding toward the trio. "May you leave nothing but footprints and take with you only happy memories."

"Thank you," Clover smiled, raising her glass to accept his tribute and taking a healthy swig of the strong wine. "And thank you for welcoming us into your home."

"It's our pleasure," Randy said, seeming to be the ringleader. "It's always a treat to socialize with newcomers outside our little clique."

"If you don't mind my asking," Tara said, ever wary of strangers. "How did you all come to live alone in this outpost so far from civilization?"

"Unfortunately," Randy said, nodding toward his friends.

"Normal people don't take kindly toward dwarves. They tend to shun and bully us, so we decided to find a place where we could be together and live in peace and solitude."

"You don't get bored, living all alone out here?" Tara said.

"Not usually," Randy smiled. "We have plenty of ways to keep ourselves amused, and we have periodic visitors who come to sample our wares."

"You mean the vegetables grown in the garden?" Clover asked.

"Among other things," Randy said, winking at his dwarf sitting next to him.

"What's the purpose of that thing in the corner?" Jessop said, staring at the ass-shaped bust. "It looks remarkably life-like."

"It's a *fucking machine*," Randy said nonchalantly. "For those lonely times when we need to feel the form of a woman."

"What's it made out of and how does it work?" Jessop said, focusing on the glistening slit under the base of the buttocks.

"Pig skin, pulled over sea sponge," Randy said. "Our group of artisans have some remarkable talents. Do you want to *touch* it?"

Jessop hesitated while he furrowed his brow at the strange contraption.

"What are those levers sticking out of the top of it?" he said, shaking his head. "What are they for?"

"The one on the right provides variable compression from wooden supports surrounding the enclosure. And the one on the left adjusts the speed of the pumping action."

"You mean that thing *moves* automatically?" Jessop said, flaring his eyes open in surprise.

"Yes," Randy said. "The internal parts are connected to a

pivot, driven by a paddlewheel connected to the outside stream. There's a cam attached to the device to adjust the speed of the movement to simulate the rocking action of a woman's pussy."

"Holy shit," Jessop said. "That's *ingenious*!"

"We thought so," Randy smiled. "Would you like to give it a try? I think you'll find it's almost as good as the real thing."

2

_____

"U m..." Jessop stammered, peering at Clover and Tara sheepishly. "I'm a little gun-shy about sticking my dick in strange places. We've been in some pretty wild situations in our travels."

"Perhaps you could provide a demonstration for us?" Clover said to Randy, feeling her pussy dampening at the idea of watching how these dwarves entertained themselves when they were horny.

"I suppose that could be arranged," Randy said, turning toward his friends assembled around the table. "Which one of you would like to show our guests how the device works?"

The dwarf introduced earlier as Itchy raised his hand with a flushed face, and Randy nodded for him to approach the apparatus. Itchy rose from the table with a large bulge in the front of his pants, then he positioned his hips in front of the skin-colored form, unhooking the flap over his crotch and pulling out an enormous, half-erect cock. Each of the friends gasped in shock, scarcely believing that such a diminutive dwarf could produce such a large phallus. He picked up a bottle of lubricating oil on the table next to the artificial pussy and as he slathered it over his organ, it hardened and lengthened, until it pointed straight out from his body a good two feet, with a girth of at least four inches. Perfectly straight, with a large bulbous head the size of a softball, it looked as large as a horse's organ on a person one-tenth its size.

Jesus, Clover muttered to herself. *Now I see why they don't use zippers or buttons on their trousers. The only possible way to free that monster is with a loose flap.*

As she stared at the dwarf's oversize organ while he massaged it to full hardness, the two women squirmed in their seats, unconsciously imagining would it would feel like to have it inside their *own* pussies. Or even if it would be possible to fit inside their pussies.

"I guess that explains why they made an artificial pussy," Tara chuckled, leaning over to whisper in Clover's ear. "I don't think that thing would *fit* anywhere else."

"Maybe not," Clover said. "But I'd sure as hell love to give it a try."

After Itchy got his dick fully hard, he grasped the end of it with two hands and pointed it toward the slit at the base of the buttocks, slowly sliding it inside the mold. As it disappeared into the machine, he groaned softly, grasping the elevated handles with his two hands. While he began to rock his hips back and forth, he slowly pulled the right lever toward him, tightening the grip of the spongy internal pussy around his throbbing organ. After he shoved his oversize balls against the back of the artificial ass, he pulled the other lever toward him, and the apparatus began to hum and shake, pumping the internal sheath back and forth over the full length of his erection. As he tipped his head backwards and moaned in pleasure, Randy turned to glance at the look of astonishment on the faces of his guests.

"Have you seen anything like this before?" he said.

"Are you referring to the *apparatus*, or the size of Itchy's cock?" Clover said.

"Both," Randy smiled.

"Neither," Clover said. "But I'd sure like to give the second one a try sometime. Are *all* of you hung like that?"

"If you're referring to the size of our organs, yes. Although Jumbo here is a little larger than the rest of us–"

"You mean it gets even bigger than *that*?" Clover said, flaring her eyes open in surprise.

"In his case, almost fifty *percent* bigger," Randy nodded.

"That's insane!" Tara chimed in. "How did you manage to grow your cocks so large?"

"We're not entirely sure," Randy said. "I suspect it's a type of inbreeding. We occasionally have sex with some of the local women and when they get pregnant, we pass along our special genes to the next generation of dwarves."

"Natural selection," Clover nodded, reflecting back to her biology class back home in Abbynthia. "Those genes that are most successful in propagating eventually come to dominate their environment."

"You must be doing a lot of *propagating* in order to ensure the success of your people," Tara smiled, watching Itchy pushing and pulling the levers above the whirring ass while he humped his hips harder against the platform.

"We get plenty of real fucking from the local women," Randy nodded. "I guess our reputation has spread around the community. The dwarves that aren't chased off find refuge in our little house in the forest."

"Now I see why the local townsmen don't want you around," Jessop said. "Besides being envious of your huge penises, you're also exceptionally fertile."

Randy paused for a moment while he glanced down at the growing bulge in Jessop's pants.

"It's odd that we've adapted bigger peckers than regularly sized people," he nodded. "Is *your* penis as small as other tall men's?"

"Well, I've been told it's a little bigger than *most*," Jessop blushed. "But nothing like the size of yours. Mine's a tadpole compared to your bullfrog-sized instruments."

"Does it still work the same way as ours?" Randy said.

"If by *work*, you mean can it get hard and make babies, then I suppose yes."

"Perhaps you'd like to sample the machine after Itchy finishes using it?" Randy smiled. "One of the nice things about fucking an artificial pussy is that you never have to worry about what happens to your seed."

"If you think it will *fit*, then absolutely," Jessop nodded excitedly, reaching under the table to straighten his hardening tool in his pants.

"We've engineered the system to accommodate organs of all sizes," Randy said, motioning toward Jumbo, who was sitting at the other end of the table. "The cams and levers are designed to work with virtually any sized cock."

"Sign me up," Jessop said, smiling toward Clover and Tara. "It's been a while since I've had any pussy, artificial or otherwise."

"We shouldn't keep our guest waiting any longer then," Randy said, elbowing the dwarf named Kinky, sitting beside him.

Kinky rose from the table then he walked over to Itchy, who was humping the artificial ass harder and faster, and reached under his legs, using his fingers to tickle the space between Itchy's balls and anus. Itchy suddenly grunted harder and leaned forward over the machine, tilting his ass upward while the other dwarf grasped his balls tightly. Itchy thrust his hips hard one last time against the shaking apparatus, squeezing his buttocks tightly together while Kinky compressed his balls as he drained his cock inside the vibrating instrument.

"Alright then," Clover chuckled as she peered over at Tara. "I guess that explains *one* dwarf's name. I can't wait to see why the *other* ones have such unusual names."

3

After Itchy pulled his huge, dripping cock out of the artificial pussy, everyone turned toward Jessop, who was eagerly awaiting his turn at the device.

"What are you waiting for?" Randy said, raising an eyebrow. "Your chariot awaits."

"Right *now*?" Jessop said. "With everybody watching?"

"That's half the fun," Randy nodded. "It's especially exciting knowing everyone else is watching your every twitch and moan. It's almost as much of a turn-on for *us* as for the one using the machine."

"What about...*cleanliness*?" Jessop said, staring at the huge pool of cum Itchy had left on the floor in front of the apparatus. "Is it safe to use it so soon after the last one?"

"The same water that drives the pumping action of the device also circulates inside it to keep it clean," Randy nodded. "As for the puddle on the floor," he said, motioning toward one of the other dwarfs. "We'll clean that up forthwith. We wouldn't want you to slip and fall in the middle of your entertainment."

The dwarf named Frisky rose from the table and cleaned the area in front of the bust with a washcloth, then he sat down on the floor a few feet further away, preparing to enjoy the show close-up.

"I should warn you," Jessop said, glancing at the other dwarfs assembled around the table. "I'm not built like the rest of you. I don't want to disappoint you with the size of my small organ..."

"We've already seen most regular-sized humans' cocks," Randy nodded. "I'm sure it will be no surprise compared to what we've seen before."

"Go ahead," Clover said, reaching under the table to squeeze Jessop's erect organ. "You know you want to give it a try. And nobody will know how big you are once you insert your tool inside the machine."

"Okay," Jessop said, slowly rising from the table. "Just don't laugh at me when you see my tiny prick."

"We wouldn't think of it," Randy smiled, glancing down at Jessop's tenting trousers. "We only want you to enjoy the experience as much as the rest of us."

Jessop walked up to the front of the machine and unzipped his pants, slowly pulling out his throbbing hard-on. He stared at the slit positioned under the anatomically correct buttocks, holding his dick tentatively in his right hand.

"Do I need to add lubrication?" he said, unsure about sticking his manhood into the humming device.

"The circulating water keeps the inside moist," Randy nodded. "But I think you'll find a little extra lubrication simulates the experience more authentically."

"*Authentic* sounds good," Jessop said, reaching for the bottle of oil sitting beside the stand and slathering it all over his bouncing cock.

"You're not as small as most of the regular humans we've met," Randy said, nodding his head appreciatively while he appraised Jessop's eight-inch-long instrument.

"Thanks, but it's a far cry from all of yours," Jessop said, pointing the tip of his penis toward the realistic-looking vulva.

"I'm pretty sure you'll enjoy the experience all the same," Randy smiled.

"Remember, it's not the *size* of the instrument that matters," Clover nodded. "It's how you use it, and we're interested to see how you find this compares to the real thing."

"I'll tell you in a few minutes," Jessop grinned, slowly inserting the tip of his cock into the machine. "Assuming this thing doesn't chop off my dick in the meantime."

But as he pressed his hips forward toward the padded cheeks of the artificial ass, the smile on his face grew progressively wider and he groaned softly.

"What do you think?" Randy said, beginning to move his arm rhythmically under the table as he massaged his own swelling organ. "Does it feel like a real pussy?"

"Yes," Jessop huffed, humping his hips slowly against the humming bust. "A little looser and softer than what I'm used to, but it feels good all the same–"

"Try pulling the right handle," Randy nodded, unhinging the flap of his britches to free his expanding hard-on.

Jessop grasped the right lever, and as he pulled it toward him, he rocked his hips harder against the machine, groaning more loudly.

"Better?" Randy said.

"Better," Jessop nodded, pulling the lever harder toward him.

"Try the *left* lever now," Randy said, pushing himself

away from the table to give his enormous erection room to stand up while he stroked it with two hands.

Before long, all of the other dwarfs had pushed back from the table to jerk their cocks in tandem with Randy while they watched Jessop's ass flexing and straining against the device. Clover and Tara stared at their gigantic phalluses, darting their eyes from one dwarf's huge erection to the next. All of them were hung similar to Itchy, who had become aroused once again watching Jessop enjoying himself at the machine, but it was Jumbo's tree-trunk-sized erection that they couldn't take their eyes off.

Standing upright almost three feet in length and six inches in diameter, it was even longer than his leg. While they stared at Jumbo and the others stroking their giant hard-ons, they reached under the table, pulling their animal-skins aside and thrusting their fingers into their pussies, fingering themselves roughly while they took in the action.

Jessop slowly reached his left hand toward the other lever and when he angled it toward him, the look on his face changed from amused distraction to unbridled bliss. While the machine began to vibrate and pulse more rapidly, he pressed his hips forward and held them tightly against the throbbing apparatus, letting the machine do all the work while he tilted his head back and savored the exquisite sensation of the pulsating device.

"Oh my God," he said, pulling both levers hard against his body as his legs began to shake.

"*Still* think it feels like a real pussy?" Randy said, gripping his swelling shaft tighter with both hands while he pumped his giant organ up and down, along with the rest of the dwarfs.

"No," Jessop grunted, squeezing his buttocks as he tried

to push his erection further into the machine. "It's even *better*. I've never felt anything like this. Not only does it feel like a real pussy, it *moves* even better. I feel like I've died and gone to heaven."

"Well, don't die too soon," Randy smiled. "Because it gets even *better*."

"Better than *this*?" Jessop said. "I can't imagine how this machine could improve the sensation any more."

"It's not only the *machine* that makes this experience better," Randy said, motioning toward Frisky, who was watching Jessop's quivering ass above his dropped trousers with growing interest. "There's a reason why seven of us live together in this small cottage. There are certain ancillary benefits to being left alone to our own devices..."

Frisky nodded toward Randy, acknowledging his instruction, then he shifted over between Jessop's parted legs and tilted his head upward, enveloping Jessop's balls between his pursed lips.

"Oh fuck, oh fuck..." Jessop hissed, tilting his hips further upward to accept the dwarf's oral ministrations.

"Better?" Randy smiled, gripping the tip of his swelling organ with his right hand while he squeezed his oversize balls with his other.

"Better," Jessop huffed, slowly arching his body forward as he moved toward the most powerful orgasm he'd ever experienced.

"Are you ready for the big finish?" Randy said, raising his hips off his chair as he prepared to climax along with Jessop.

"Yes, yes, yes," Jessop grunted, swinging the two levers back and forth wildly while Frisky slurped his tightening balls.

Frisky raised his head a few inches higher, darting his tongue in and out of Jessop's puckering anus, and Jessop made a sound like a wild animal while he emptied his load inside the machine, clamping his anus around Frisky's undulating tongue while he experienced one long contraction after another. Meanwhile, when the rest of the dwarves around the table saw that Jessop had reached the height of his pleasure, they raised their cocks together in unison, gripping them tightly while they sprayed their jism high above the table in a coordinated display of erotic delight, like some kind of sperm fountain.

When Clover and Tara saw the dwarfs' enormous cocks erupting in unison, they leaned forward unconsciously, jerking their bodies under the spray while they rammed their fingers deep inside their convulsing pussies. For both of the women, it had been the most exciting and arousing show they'd ever witnessed, and each of them was dying to get a piece of the action when everybody recovered from this latest spectacle.

4

"Oh my God," Clover gushed after she and Tara recovered from their orgasms. "That was *insane!*"

"Are you talking about the dwarves' huge *cocks*, or the amount of spunk they just dropped on us?" Tara said, wiping the streams of splooge off her face.

"Both," Clover panted.

"What about you, Jessop?" Randy said, licking the last dribbles of cum off the top of his dick with his tongue. "Did you enjoy your turn with the artificial pussy?"

"Fuck yes," Jessop said, reluctantly pulling his dripping dick out of the humming apparatus and nodding toward Frisky, who was licking his lips after slurping Jessop's balls. "I don't know if sex is ever going to be the same again after trying this machine."

"There's nothing quite like doing it with a real person," Randy said. "The machine can simulate the feeling of a woman's pussy, but it can't mimic her reactions and the feeling of connection with another person."

"Speaking of sex with another person," Clover said. "Tara

and I are eager to sample the real thing this time. I don't suppose one of you would like to give *me* a try instead of stroking your own cocks? That is, assuming you've still got enough energy left after spilling your loads all over our heads."

"Let's see," Randy said, peering around the table at the flagging erections of the other dwarfs. "Who's up for another go with one of our guests?"

Every one of the dwarfs quickly shot up their hands, and Randy chuckled while he appraised the turgidity of their cocks.

"It looks like Splashy wins the award for fastest recovery time," he said, peering at the dwarf's twitching tool. "How would you like to do this, exactly?"

Clover peered at Splashy's enormous instrument, then she turned toward Tara, wrinkling her forehead.

"Don't look at *me* for suggestions," Tara chuckled. "I'm just as perplexed as you as to how you're going to fit that thing inside you."

Clover paused for a moment while she considered her options, then she nodded slowly.

"I think it's better if I take the *superior* position," she said. "That way I can better control where and how much he penetrates me."

"Okay," Randy said, motioning toward Splashy. "Why don't you lie down in the middle of the floor with your cock facing up, so the lady can take her time figuring out how to fully appreciate our endowments?"

Splashy nodded toward Randy, then he rose from the table and lay down on the floor as the senior dwarf had instructed, with little rivulets of precum spilling out the tip of his cock and streaming down the sides of his upturned shaft.

"Why do they call him *Splashy*?" Clover said, squinting at the copious amount of fluid he was emitting from his cock.

"You're about to find out," Randy grinned. "But I assure you, it won't be anything disagreeable. In fact, I think you'll find his special talents quite refreshing."

"Okay," Clover said, walking over to Splashy's position on the floor and kneeling between his legs while she stared at his throbbing tool. "Can I *touch* it? I've never handled a cock anywhere near this big before."

"Mm-hmm," Splashy hummed, flexing his buttocks to lift his hips higher off the floor.

"Mmm," Clover purred, reaching out both of her hands to squeeze his thick shaft and slowly rubbing them up and down. "That is one impressive piece of meat you have there. That thing could feed an entire family for a week."

"I don't think he'd appreciate you chopping it up into smaller pieces," Randy laughed. "But I'm sure he would mind if you *licked* it as an appetizer."

"Yes," Clover said, tilting her head down to taste Splashy's precum still streaming down the sides of his organ.

She flicked her tongue over his bobbing crown, then she purred with a big smile on her face.

"It tastes like *honey*," she nodded, turning toward Tara. "Not nearly as salty as Jessop's cum."

"That's okay," Jessop said sarcastically. "Because I can use the fucking machine now, which does a better job anyway."

"I'm glad you like it," Randy chuckled. "Because there's a lot more where that came from."

"I'm intrigued," Clover said while she traced the tip of her tongue under the rim of the dwarf's throbbing frenulum. "With your penises as large as they are, it would appear you can suck your *own* cocks as easily as anyone else. Why did you choose to stroke them with your hands while Jessop was using the machine instead of sucking yourself off instead?"

"Oh, we *do*, believe me," Randy smiled. "It's just that in this case, we wanted to keep our heads up so we could enjoy watching all of you coming along with us."

"Makes sense," Clover nodded. "Though I'm interested to watch *that* sometime soon too. I've never seen a guy sucking his own dick before."

"We'll be happy to oblige soon enough," Randy said, glancing at his compatriot squirming on the floor. "But something tells me that Splashy is enjoying your oral attention a lot more than he would his own."

"Hmm," Clover said, lifting her head to appraise the size of the dwarf's bulbous crown. "I'm not even sure I could get my lips all the way around that thing. I don't know if I'll be able to give him a proper blow job–"

"It takes a bit of training to stretch your lips, but eventually most of the women seem to figure it out. Although Splashy seems to be enjoying what you're doing plenty enough right now."

Clover paused for a moment while she examined the full anatomy of the dwarf's genitalia, darting her eyes all the way up from his huge, oversize balls to his flaring helmet-shaped crown.

"It's amazing how similar your instruments are to a normal man's cock," she nodded, twisting her palms gently around the base of Splashy's glans while he moaned softly on the floor. "It's shaped exactly the same, only four times the size. It reminds me of those old Japanese shunga woodblocks..."

"Woodblocks?" Randy said, wrinkling his forehead.

"They're hand-carved paintings from my time," Clover

said. "I always found them incredibly arousing, and here I am, *touching* one in the flesh."

"He seems to be enjoying it," Randy nodded.

"Let's see if he enjoys *this* even more," Clover smiled, lowering her head over Splashy's glans and stretching her lips as wide as she could, trying to slip him into her mouth.

It took a few minutes of pressing and squeezing to get his crown into her cavity, and after she did, she was only able to twist her head over his tip instead of bobbing up and down or using her tongue to provide extra stimulation. Nonetheless, Splashy seemed to enjoy her technique, humping her face softly while her head bounced up and down atop his pumping flagpole.

"Unghh," he groaned, grabbing the back of her head, trying to force her further down his cock.

But Clover resisted his pressure and she raised her head, popping his dick out of her mouth.

"Whoa there, skippy," she said, wiping the copious precum from around the edges of her mouth. "You're going to *suffocate* me with that thing if I go any lower."

"It's *Splashy*," Randy said, correcting Clover's misnomer.

"Yeah, I know," Clover nodded. "It's just that, given the nature of his boyish excitement, maybe you should consider giving him a new name."

"We'll have to see about that," Randy said. "You still haven't experienced what he's most famous for."

"Why don't we try this a different way?" Clover said, standing up and positioning her pussy over his dripping organ. "I've got a feeling that my *lower* lips might be a little more flexible. And I'll be in better control, being out of reach of his outstretched arms."

Tara cleared her throat as she watched the fountain of

precum spewing out of Splashy's dick while Clover squatted closely above him.

"What about the *pregnancy* issue?" she said, temporarily interrupting Clover's well-intentioned plan. "Remember what Randy said earlier about how fertile they are? You don't want to spit out another dwarf in nine months, like some of the other village women."

"Good point," Clover nodded. "I don't suppose you keep a stock of condoms nearby, do you?"

"What are *condoms*?" Randy said, peering at Clover with a confused expression.

"They're little plastic things you put over your dick to keep women from getting–" Then she interrupted herself, shaking her head. "Yeah, I guess that's not something you worry about very much with seven men occupying the same house. Besides, you'd never find anything big enough to stretch over your huge penises, anyway."

"If you're referring to a semen blocker," Randy said. "Sometimes we wrap the same kind of pig skin used inside the artificial pussy to wrap our organs when we have sex with women from the village. It's a bit of a crude protection, but it seems to work most of the time."

"I'm willing to give it a try if you have a little extra lying around," Clover said, beginning to drip her own juices over the tip of Splashy's flaring instrument in anticipation of feeling his dick inside her.

Randy got up from the table and opened a drawer in a nearby commode, then he handed Clover a two-foot-square piece of fabric. Clover rubbed her fingers over the texture of the thin translucent skin, then she nodded her head.

"It looks sturdy enough," she said, placing it gently overtop Splashy's unturned pole like a tent canvas.

Then she slowly lowered her hips over the tip of his

covered cock, groaning while she flexed her legs and relaxing her Kegel muscles, feeling him slowing entering her hole.

"Holy *shit*," she said, rolling her eyes backward in her head. "That feels incredible."

"Is it going *inside*?" Tara said, straining forward to watch the couple on the floor.

"Slowly," Clover grunted. "But exquisitely. I've never felt anything like this before. This is the biggest thing I've had up my pussy since that turn with the centaur in the woods. And this one is connected to a real human this time."

"See how much of him you can take," Tara nodded, noticing the cocks of the other dwarves beginning to rise again while they watched the show unfolding in the middle of there living room.

Tara lowered her body a little further, and Splashy groaned while he watched her tits bobbing gently on her chest.

"You *like* that, Splashy?" Clover said, peering down at his flushing face.

"Un-huh," the dwarf huffed, holding the base of his huge dick with two hands to steady it while Clover rocked her body awkwardly over his supine body.

"Me too," Clover said, flexing her thigh muscles while she bobbed atop his organ, now almost halfway embedded inside her pussy.

By now, all of the other dwarves and even Jessop were fully hard while they jacked their upturned cocks as they watched Clover fucking the happy dwarf lying on the floor. Tara noticed the dwarf named Noisy licking the tip of his instrument while he tilted his head to the side trying to take in the action, and she rose from her seat, kneeling between his legs.

"Why don't you let me help you with that?" she said, stretching her lips over his flaring glans while she grasped his thick pole with two hands. "You enjoy the show while I take care of your other needs."

By now, Clover was nearing the peak her of excitement as she bounced atop Splashy's enormous erection, with the lips of her vulva stretched so tightly over his thick organ that the base of her clit rubbed up against the side of his pulsating shaft.

"Fuck, that feels good," she cooed, staring into Splashy's face while his mouth began to widen as he neared his own climax. "*Come* with me, Splashy. I'm going to gush all over your huge pecker..."

"Yes, yes," Splashy panted, stroking the base of his pole while Clover squeezed her pussy over the upper portion of his hard-on.

Suddenly, she began squealing and shaking while she squirted her juices down the shaft of Splashy's cock, and he contorted his face into a tight grimace when he felt her spray washing over his balls. Without warning, Clover's body jetted off the top of his erupting instrument as the force of his enormous ejaculation held back by the improvised condom literally blew her two feet into the air. At the same time, all the other dwarves around the table climaxed one after another, with Noisy making the loudest noise of all as his semen gushed out the sides of Tara's stretched mouth, still impaled around his organ.

"Eeeeiii!" he screamed, holding Tara's face over his cock until he emptied his seed into her overflowing cavity.

By the time everyone had finished coming from the excitement of the erotic show in the middle of the floor, the entire place was coated in semen, all the way from the floor to the rafters. Clover braced her legs on the slippery floor while her muscles quivered in post-orgasmic exhaustion, trying not to slip on the river of fluid under her feet.

"Well, I guess we know how *Splashy* got his name," she grinned, glancing over toward Tara, who was flexing her sore jaw after detaching from Noisy's dripping dick.

"Not to mention *Noisy*," she grinned. "I thought he was going to blow my head *clean off* when he came in my mouth."

"That just leaves Kinky, Randy, and Jumbo to decipher," Clover chuckled.

"I wouldn't worry about *Jumbo*," Tara smiled, staring at his throbbing cock standing at least a foot above all the others. "I've got something special in mind for him at our next turn around the table."

5

After the dwarves cleaned up the mess they'd left on the floor and the table, Tara took off her deer-skin suit and lay on the floor where Splashy had been, beckoning for Jumbo to join her.

"It's *my* turn to play the passive role," she smiled, spreading her legs apart to show Jumbo her glistening pussy.

Jumbo peered at the diminutive elf lying sexily on the floor while his enormous cock began to lengthen and rise above his stout body.

"I'm pretty sure I won't be able to fit inside that little slit," he said, shaking his head.

"Don't worry, I had something *else* in mind," Tara said, curling her fingers toward him in a come-hither motion. "Kneel in front of me while you lay that thumper on my belly. I want you to tit-fuck me while I feel your big balls rubbing against my pussy. Then I'm going to massage your beautiful tip with my hands and watch you come on my face."

"That sounds *hot*," Jumbo nodded as his big dick continued rising until it pointed above his head.

"Grab some oil next to the fucking machine," Tara said when she saw that he was ready. "This is going to be a whole lot more interesting that sticking your dick in an artificial pussy."

Jumbo picked up the bottle of oil next to the machine and slathered it over his long schlong, rubbing his hands up and down his shaft to spread it evenly.

"I don't think *two hands* is going to cut it," Tara smiled, motioning for him to kneel in front of her. "Let's see what it feels like when I wrap my arms and legs around it."

"Fuck yes," Jumbo said, kneeling between Tara's parted legs and slapping his organ down onto her stomach with a loud plop.

"Oomph!" Tara grunted when she felt the full weight of his cactus-sized erection.

But as he began to slide it up her belly between her plump tits, and she felt his grapefruit-sized balls grinding against her throbbing clit, she wrapped her arms around his swelling organ and pulled it hard against her oil-covered chest. When his giant glans bounced against her chin, she placed both of her hands around his rim and twisted her palms, causing Jumbo to groan in pleasure.

"I bet your friends can't do *this*," she said, squeezing her breasts against the side of his pumping shaft. "Or this," she grinned, lifting her knees and criss-crossing her legs around the base of his shaft while pulling his balls harder against her dripping pussy.

By now, she had a death grip on his enormous organ, squeezing it tightly between her arms and legs while she humped her hips against his tightening balls and massaged the head of his dick like she was polishing a door knob.

"That feels incredible," Jumbo grunted, watching his glistening organ slide between Tara's tits while she caressed his sensitive glans. "You're so *wet*..."

"Not as wet as *you* are," Tara said, feeling his precum mixing with the oil from the side table to create a perfect lubricant.

She flicked her tongue over the slit on the end of his penis and nodded toward Clover.

"I see what you mean, Clover," she said. "Their sperm does taste sweet and delicious. Forget about *eating* their dicks. Their *milk* alone could sustain us for as long as we want."

"Maybe," Clover chuckled. "But watch out when he comes. These dwarves' ejaculations pack a powerful punch. I wouldn't want him to knock you out when he climaxes."

"You wouldn't do that to me, would you Jumbo?" Tara said, pinching her eyebrows together like a puppy dog while she peered up at the hung dwarf. "Will you give me a warning when you're about to come? At least so I can catch my breath so I don't suffocate in your tsunami of semen."

"Okay," Jumbo grunted, sliding his big dick harder between her arms and tits. "It won't be long now. I can feel the pressure building up in my balls."

"Good," Tara nodded. "Push them harder against my pussy. They're stimulating my clit better than any regular-sized cock ever could."

"Fuck, yes," he growled, tilting his hips harder against her crotch while she tightened her hold on his swelling glans. "I'm going to come any second now."

"That's it, big boy," Tara purred, feeling her own orgasm welling up inside her stomach. "Come all over me. Let me watch you shoot your spunk all over my face."

"*Yes, yes,*" Jumbo huffed, until he rammed his totem

against her belly one last time, raising his face upwards while he let out a deep growl. *"Nngahhh!"*

Tara tilted her head backwards just in time to watch his thick ropes of cum shooting over her face in streams as thick as a garden hose, one after another while she squeezed her thighs over his pulsating organ, jerking her convulsing pussy against his balls while she climaxed in tandem with him. It took almost a full minute for the two of them to finish shaking overtop one another, and when they finally finished coming, Jumbo collapsed onto the floor beside Tara, tilting his throbbing dick into the air while everyone else looked on in rapt attention.

Tara raised her head and peered at the group sitting around the table, watching them holding their dripping dicks in their hands while they glanced back at the duo with flushed faces.

"You guys sure have a lot of stamina for a bunch of *little people*," she said. "No wonder the local village women come out here for some personal entertainment from time to time. They can always count on at least *one* of you ready to satisfy whatever needs they might have."

"They don't give us names like Randy and Kinky for nothing," Randy chuckled, sliding his fingers over his swelling helmet. "We might be small in stature, but our *libidos* match the size of our cocks."

"That's good to know," Tara smiled. "Because you're the only two who haven't yet had a turn putting on a show."

"How should we pair them up?" Clover said, pulling her fingers out of her dripping pussy.

"I don't know about you," Tara said. "But I'm eager to see what they do when they play amongst themselves. Are you two willing to put on a little demonstration while the rest of us watch from the sidelines?"

Randy paused while he turned toward his seatmate and smiled.

"What do you say, Kinky?" he said. "Are you ready for a little more action?"

"Always," Kinky smiled, spilling a drop of dew out of the top of his dick in anticipation of his sexy guests watching them share in the fun. "As long as I can have a turn with one of the others later in the evening."

"There's plenty of us to go around," Tara said, glancing at her friends still fondling their genitals under the table. "I think even *Jessop* is willing to give it another go. What do you say, Jessop? Do you want to try a little *boy-on-boy* action next time?"

"I'm not exactly sure how I'll be able to keep up with these guys," he nodded, stroking his half-erect cock under the table. "But I've been dying to *touch* one of those monsters ever since I saw Itchy fucking the artificial pussy."

"Save that thought," Tara smiled, rising up from the floor and wiping herself down with a towel while the other two dwarfs took her place in the middle of the living room.

6

Randy and Kinky walked to the center of the room with their half-erect penises wobbling in front of them, then they sat down facing one another, bending their knees so their balls touched together. At first, they just slapped their dicks together like they were playfully jousting, but after they got fully hard and their cocks pointed straight up, they grabbed each other's organs with two hands and started pumping them up and down. While the rest of the group looked on from the nearby table, the other dwarves mimicked their movement, stroking their cocks with two hands.

Clover, Tara, and Jessop seemed fascinated by the manner in which they played with their tools, preferring to hump their dicks over their hands rather than moving their hands directly. Once in a while, after their precum dribbled down the sides of their flaring crowns, they'd grasp their glans, twisting their hands from side to side while they moaned softly.

"Do you wish you had a cock that big?" Clover said to Jessop, who was darting his eyes from one dwarf's hard-on to another while he pistoned his hand rapidly over his own erection.

"Damn straight," he nodded as he reveled in the sight of the seven dwarfs stroking their giant organs.

"Because it would make you feel more *manly*?" Tara said, circling her clit while she watched all the action.

"Not so much that as there's just so much more to play with," Jessop said, squeezing his balls with his left hand while he stroked his crown with his right hand. "If the size of their cocks mirrors the amount of nerve endings they have down there, it must feel four times as good as mine."

"Possibly," Clover nodded, reaching over to tickle his perineum while he fapped his dick. "But wouldn't you also like the chance to *suck* your own dick?"

"Fuck, yes," Jessop grunted, resisting the urge to lean over and slurp the upturned pole of the dwarf sitting next to him. "Though I'm not sure I'd be able to fit it inside my mouth."

"It's not as hard as it looks," Clover said. "It just takes a bit of patience and practice. But once you do, it's an incredible sensation. Plus, their cum tastes delicious."

"I'll have to take your word for it," Jessop said, watching the tips of Randy's and Kinky's erections dripping like an overflowing volcano while they rubbed their two cocks together.

As if on cue, the two dwarfs leaned their heads forward, engulfing each other's tool in their mouths while they continued stroking their own instruments.

"*Fuck*, that's hot," Clover said, abandoning her attempt to make Jessop feel more comfortable and returning her hands to her own pussy, ramming two fingers inside her dripping cunt while she rubbed her clit with her other hand.

"I don't even know why they *bother* with the artificial

pussy," Tara said, squeezing her tits while she trilled her clit. "With seven hung dwarfs inside this place, the possibilities seem endless."

"So it would seem," Clover said, noticing the two dwarves in the middle of the room grunting louder and more urgently as their faces reddened in rising excitement.

Suddenly, they pulled their bobbing heads off each other's pricks at the same time, gasping loudly while their dicks bobbed together on the brink of climax.

"Why didn't you *finish*?" Clover said, peering toward Randy, whose chest was still heaving from the intense pleasure.

"Sometimes it's more fun bringing ourselves to the *edge,* then backing off," Randy said, smiling toward Kinky. "This way, we can make it last longer and enjoy the feeling of dancing on the edge of orgasm."

"Yes," Tara nodded, pausing the stimulation of her own clit while she caught her breath. "I like to edge for long periods sometimes too, while I'm stimulating myself. It's a lovely indulgence when you're in the right mood and you've got no distractions to divert your attention."

"I agree," Clover nodded, raising her feet onto the top of the table and spreading her knees far apart while she peered down at her swelling labia and her leaking pussy dripping rivers of fluid down the crack of her ass. "Take as much time as you like. I'm in no hurry to come, and I'm enjoying the show tremendously."

"Me too," Jessop said, watching his organ twitching between his legs.

"You might want to save yourself for the next round," Clover chuckled, noticing his precum dribbling out of his slit and coating the top of his purple crown. "That is, if you want to have your *own* turn with one of the dwarfs once Randy and Kinky finish their little tete-a-tete."

"Oh, I want a *turn* alright," Jessop smiled. "I don't know exactly what I'm going to do with them, but I'm dying to feel one of those monsters close-up."

Suddenly, the dwarf sitting next to Jessop stopped stroking his dick as he elbowed Jessop gently in his side.

"You can stroke *mine* if you feel like saving yourself for later," Frisky said. "Or even better, *suck* me so I can watch Randy and Kinky pleasing each other."

"Really?" Jessop said, flaring his eyes open in excitement. "I wouldn't mind returning the favor you gave me earlier while I was fucking the machine. Your tongue licking my balls and anus made the experience a hundred times better."

"Knock yourself out," Frisky smiled. "Just be careful when I come. I wouldn't want you to *gag* from my huge volume of fluid."

"If it's as tasty as Clover and Tara lead me to believe, it'll be my pleasure," Jessop said, lowering his head onto Frisky's twitching hard-on and circling his tongue slowly around his sensitive glans.

"What do you *think*?" Tara said, watching Jessop humming in delight while he slathered Frisky's helmet with his tongue.

"Mmm," he nodded. "It's sweet and creamy, kind of like an ice cream cone."

"Lick the sides of my crown and see if you can keep the cream from spilling over the edge," Frisky said.

"Yes," Jessop hummed while he slurped Frisky's big organ. "This is better than an ice cream cone. It *tastes* just as good, but it's a thousand times more fun."

"That goes for *two* of us," Frisky moaned, rocking his hips up and down while Jessop licked his swelling head.

"See if you can get your mouth all the way around it," Clover nodded, slipping her fingers back into her pussy. "You should have less trouble than Tara and me with your bigger mouth."

"Hmm," Jessop said, staring at Frisky's huge organ then lowering his head over the tip of his dick while he stretched his lips and slowly took him into his mouth.

"Nnngh," Frisky grunted when the tip of his dick slipped inside Jessop's mouth. "Your mouth is much tighter than the other dwarves. I'm going to blow my load soon. My balls are starting to tingle."

When Randy and Kinky saw their friend being sucked off by Jessop, they lowered their heads once again and resumed sucking each other's dicks, this time rubbing their poles together while they wrapped their hands around their joined cocks, groaning more vigorously while their their balls slowly tightened. Clover and Tara rammed their fingers back inside their cunts, then the remaining four dwarfs paired up, leaning over to suck one another's cocks while the room began to fill with the sound of loud moaning and grunting.

"Fuck this," Tara huffed, climbing on top of the table and spreading her legs in front of Clover's face. "I could use an oral fix of my own. Do you feel like giving the boys a little show of while we lick each other's pussies?"

"In the *sixty-nine* position?" Clover said, smiling up at her while she stared at her dripping pussy.

"Yes," Tara smiled, resting her head onto the table and motioning for her friend to climb on top of her. "We don't have the anatomical advantage of our horse-sized friends. But something tells me they'll enjoy the spectacle of watching two women going down on each other just the same."

"I'm way ahead of you," Clover nodded, climbing up onto the table on all fours and positioning her pussy over Tara's face while she lowered her head between the elf's thighs.

"Oh my God," Noisy rasped next to them when he saw the two women writhing their bodies together, inches away from his throbbing cock. "I've never seen two women do it like that."

"Neither have I," Splashy said, sitting two seats away while their seatmates bobbed their heads atop their flaring pricks, glancing out of the corner of their eyes while they jerked their cocks as they watched Clover and Tara licking each other.

"Mmhm-hmm," Randy and Kinky groaned from the center of the room as they peered at the spectacle unfolding on the table while they sucked each other's cocks.

Within a couple of minutes, the entire room was filled with the sound of loud moaning and grunting as everyone neared orgasm. When Frisky was the first to pop off, Jessop's eyes widened when he felt the dwarf's semen erupting in his mouth, fighting to keep a grip on his swelling glans while his jism jetted out the sides of his mouth as he gulped down the nectar.

"Oh fuck, oh fuck," Noisy screamed as he jetted his own spunk in his partner's mouth while the two women began shaking and squealing atop the table.

Seconds later, the entire room erupted into a symphony of moans and groans while everyone climaxed hard watching each other have the most erotic experience of their lives.

7

After everybody climaxed and cleaned up after themselves, all eyes turned to Jessop, who was still hard and excited after sucking off Frisky.

"Poor baby," Clover said, staring at his twitching cock. "You didn't come along with the rest of us?"

"I was too busy trying not to choke on Frisky's load," Jessop laughed. "That was a lot more than I could handle."

"It looks like you could use a little help with that," Tara said, noticing his cock glistening with precum. "You're still the only one who hasn't officially had a turn with one of the dwarves."

"We'd be happy to oblige," Randy nodded, rejoining the others around the table while he wiped the last traces of Kinky's cum from around the edges of his mouth. "What do you feel like doing? We could suck you off, or maybe you'd like to fuck one of us up the ass? Our cocks are a little too big for us to do that directly."

"That's not really my thing," Jessop said, staring at the dripping instruments of the seven dwarfs seated around the table. "I'd just like to *touch* one of those things..."

"Did you have anyone specifically in mind?" Randy said, noticing the other dwarfs' tools beginning to thicken again at the prospect of their guest getting more involved in the action.

Jessop paused as his eyes darted around the table, appraising each of the dwarf's swelling organs, then his gaze stopped when he noticed Jumbo's pole standing a foot above all the others.

"The bigger, the better," he smiled, spilling a drop of precum over his throbbing glans as he imagined handling Jumbo's enormous phallus.

"What did you have in mind, exactly?" Jumbo said, glancing at Jessop's relatively small organ. "There's no way you'd be able to get your mouth around my cock, and your tool is barely big enough to even *frot* with me."

"Can I just...*touch* it with my hands?" Jessop said, his cock bobbing in excitement at the idea of caressing the dwarf's enormous organ.

"Of course," Jumbo said, pushing his chair back from the table to expose his entire genitalia. "I've never had a regular man touch me down there. I'm intrigued to see what you can do with my equipment."

Jessop walked over to Jumbo's chair and positioned himself between his legs, then he reached out to touch his giant glans with two hands, squeezing his spongy head as he slid his fingers around the perimeter.

"It's *huge*," Jessop nodded, as his cock bobbed in excitement while he caressed the hung dwarf. "But it otherwise feels just like a regular cock."

"Only five times the *size*," Clover laughed, placing her fingers over Tara's dripping pussy under the table as she became increasingly turned on watching her friend playing with the freakishly large dwarf.

"I can't even imagine what it must feel like when you come," Jessop nodded as he caressed Jumbo's twitching glans. "I'm surprised you don't *faint* from all the blood draining from the rest of your body when you get an erection."

"I seem to have gotten used to it over the years," Jumbo chuckled as Jessop continued to play with his swelling corona. "But I sometimes get lightheaded when I stay hard for too long."

"Is there something I can do to help you get off more quickly?" Jessop said. "Because I'm enjoying just playing with this beautiful prick..."

"I wouldn't want *you* to miss out on any of the fun," Jumbo smiled, watching Jessop's tiny dick bobbing in excitement as he massaged the dwarf's much larger instrument. "Why don't you try sticking that thing *inside* me?"

"I'm not really into anal," Jessop said. "I just like touching and frotting other guys' cocks."

"It wouldn't be much fun rubbing our different-sized dicks together," Jumbo said, noticing a drop of precum spilling out of the slit of Jessop's pecker. "But I've got an idea if you like rubbing cocks together. Why don't you try sticking yours inside my *pee-hole*?"

Jessop's eyes suddenly flared as he stared at Jumbo's spasming slit and the copious amount of fluid spilling out of the tip.

"Do you think it would *fit* in there?" he said, almost coming at the thought of docking his cock with the dwarf's giant erection.

"There's only one way to find out," Jumbo nodded, staring at the string of precum hanging off the end of Jessop's throbbing organ. "We're both producing plenty of lubrication to facilitate the insertion."

"That's *insane*," Jessop said, unable to take his eyes off the dwarf's puckering opening, almost the size of a regular woman's pussy.

"Your *cock* doesn't seem to think so," Tara laughed while Jessop shifted his erection closer to Jumbo's organ. "Why don't you give it a try? It's probably just as tight as a woman's pussy, and you already said you like touching other guy's cocks. This is about as close as you can possibly get without actually fucking them up the ass."

"Okay," Jessop said, pinching the tip of his dick with the fingers of his right hand and steering it toward Jumbo's dripping orifice.

When he pressed it against the dwarf's glans, Jumbo's slit slowly widened while Jessop's pecker began to slip inside.

"Ohhh," he groaned as his dick started sliding inside the dwarf's much larger organ.

"Feel *good*?" Clover said, slipping her fingers inside Tara's pussy while she jilled herself under the table.

"You have no idea," Jessop panted, slowly pressing his hard-on further inside Jumbo's thick instrument as the dwarf began to stroke his own shaft slowly with two hands. "It feels a bit like a woman's pussy, only a lot tighter."

"Try putting it in all the way," Tara panted as Clover began to finger her harder. "That is so hot."

"No shit," Randy said, stroking his newly invigorated erection with both hands while the rest of the dwarves joined in next to him, staring at the docked couple, transfixed. "I hope you've got enough left over afterward to fuck the *rest* of us, because I've never seen anything like that."

"Fuck *yes*," Jessop panted, slapping his hips against the tip of Jumbo's flagpole while he buried his dick all the way inside his throbbing organ. "This is way better than fucking the machine. Jumbo's dick is much sexier, plus it gives me something to hold onto while I'm fucking him."

Jessop placed his two hands around the dwarf's pole and slid his palms back and forth along his shaft as he began to pick up the pace of his rocking motion. Meanwhile, Jumbo slowly arched his hips upward as he tilted his head backward, reveling in the feeling of the smaller dick stimulating the inside of his organ.

"Does that feel good, Jumbo?" Randy asked, unable to take his eyes off the duo, fucking only inches away from the rest of the mesmerized dwarfs.

"It's *incredible*," Jumbo said as Jessop slid his hands over his swelling crown. "It feels twice as good as getting a regular handjob. I'm going to spew all over Jessop's dick any second..."

"It's probably similar to stimulating the G-spot inside a woman's pussy," Tara nodded as Clover began to curl her fingers against the front wall of her tunnel. "There's just as many nerve endings on the *inside* as the outside."

"I'm glad you guys helped us discover it," Jumbo grunted, raising his hips higher above his chair as he neared the brink of orgasm. "This is definitely going to be a new technique the rest of us will incorporate into our regular routine."

"Oh my God," Jessop suddenly groaned, grasping the tip of Jumbo's swelling helmet as he thrust his dick hard inside the dwarf's dripping slit. "I'm going to come so hard..."

"Me too," Jumbo gasped, squeezing his balls while he yawned his mouth open in rising pleasure. "Here it comes–"

Suddenly, a giant eruption of cum spewed out every side of his erupting crown while Jessop's hips quivered against his purple glans, with both of the men gripping the dwarf's convulsing hard-on as Jessop drained his seed inside

Jumbo's throbbing instrument. Unable to resist the sight of the two men joined in ecstasy at the side of the table, one by one each of the dwarfs shot their own loads high into the air above the table in a cascade of glistening spunk while Tara and Clover jerked their bodies in blissful unison, coming simultaneously along with the rest of the group.

"Fuck, that was hot," Tara panted after she and Tara came down from their climaxes, with their fingers still deeply embedded inside their throbbing pussies. "I can't imagine how we're going to top that one. I've never seen anything so erotic in my entire life."

"Suddenly, there was a soft tap on the front door of the cottage, and Randy squinted at the other dwarves with a curious expression.

"Are you expecting *company*?" Clover said, pinching her eyebrows at the rest of the dwarves.

"Not that we know of," Randy said, pushing back from the table. "But sometimes we get visits from the village maidens, looking for a little side action."

"Well, by all means, let them in," Clover smiled. "The more the merrier. We could use a few more *pussies* around here to keep up with all this testosterone."

8

Randy pulled on his pants and walked over to the front door, swinging it open to reveal three beautiful young women, barely out of their teens. They peered down at the big bulge in his trousers, then giggled softly between themselves.

"May I help you?" he said, darting his eyes over their tight corsets and swelling breasts.

"We heard you dwarves enjoy some female companionship from time to time," one of the girls said.

"It must get awfully lonely out here all by yourselves," the second one smiled.

"We're not allowed to fraternize with the men from the village before we're married," the third one nodded.

"Well, we have no such restrictions here," Randy said, opening the door to welcome the girls inside. "Although we do have some guests presently, you're welcome to join us for a while."

The girls stepped inside the cottage and glanced at the other dwarves and the three friends who were hastily pulling on their clothes, then they nodded knowingly amongst themselves.

"There's no need to stop whatever you were doing," the first girl said. "We're happy to *watch* if you were in the middle of something."

"I'm sure we can keep you better entertained than that," Randy smiled. "What are your names?"

"Sara, Clara, and Tara," the first girl said, pointing toward herself and her two companions.

"My name's Randy," the senior dwarf said. "And these are my housemates Frisky, Itchy, Kinky, Splashy, Noisy, and Jumbo. And those are our guests, Clover, Tara, and Jessop."

The girl named Tara peered at her namesake and widened her eyes, noticing Tara's pointed ears.

"Are you an *elf*?" she said, running her eyes over Tara's tight-fitting animal skin bodysuit.

"Yes," Tara huffed, crossing her arms over her chest defensively. "Do you have a *problem* with that?"

"Definitely not," the other Tara said. "It's just that I've never seen one up close before. You're much sexier than I imagined."

"You're not so bad, yourself," Tara nodded, glancing at her long legs and tight bosom.

"Would you girls like something to eat?" Randy said, motioning toward the pot still resting on the stove. "We've still got a bit of rabbit stew left over–"

"We're hungry for a *different* kind of meat," Clara grinned, glancing at the seven dwarves' swelling crotches. "We heard you dwarves have some unique features you don't mind sharing with the local village women from time-to-time..."

"If you're referring to our larger-than-normal *penises*,

we'd be happy to oblige," Randy said, nodding toward his eager friends.

"Mmm," Sara hummed, stepping closer to Randy and caressing his swelling cock under his pants. "But there's *seven* of you and only three of us. How could we possibly satisfy all of you at the same time?"

Randy paused for a moment while he darted his eyes between his housemates and the new guests.

"I have an idea if you're willing to try something different. One of the dwarves is hung a little better than the rest of us. Jumbo could lay on the floor while the five women sit on his lap in a circle, rubbing their pussies against his big cock while you service the rest of us with your mouths."

The girls paused for a moment, then they glanced toward Jessop.

"What about the *boy*?" Clara said. "Plus, that still leaves one other dwarf still unattended."

"I've got an idea how I can keep him entertained," Randy smiled. "That is, if you girls don't mind sharing Jumbo's big prick–"

The three village girls turned toward Jumbo, who had unhinged the flap of his trousers, revealing his enormous instrument, rising slowly above his belly.

"*Fuck* no," Tara said, widening her eyes in shock while she peered at his huge phallus. "That thing is big enough for *all* of us."

Jumbo kicked off his breeches then he sauntered over to the middle of the room, lying down in a spread-eagle position on the floor with his thick organ pointed up in the air.

"Why don't you make yourselves more comfortable?" Randy smiled, motioning for them to sit in his lap.

The girls stared at one another for a moment then they quickly nodded, tearing off their smocks and undergarments, throwing them in a pile on the floor. Then they slowly approached Jumbo's upturned erection, stroking it gently while they squatted down around its base, holding on to his firm shaft for support.

"Have you got room for two *more*?" Clover said, grinning at the three girls.

"I'm pretty sure we can squeeze you in," Sara nodded, staring at her shaved pussy. "This thing is as big as a tree trunk!"

"Except it's a lot softer and *tastier*," Tara the elf grinned, taking a seat beside the three girls along with Clover, while the five women interlaced their legs and wrapped them around Jumbo's upturned pole like the tentacles of an octopus.

"Oh my God," he groaned, rolling his eyes back in his head. "I've never had five women ride my cock at the same time before."

"What about five women *licking* it at the same time?" Clover grinned, motioning for the other girls to lean forward and slurp the underside of his flaring glans from five different angles.

"Holy *fuck*," Jumbo grunted, spilling a thick drop of cream out of the slit atop his glans. "That feels incredible."

"It *tastes* pretty good, too," Clara nodded, nodding her head up and down while she lapped up his spilling honey.

"Mmm," the other Tara said, slurping his flaring crown along with the other girls. "I could eat this stuff all day..."

"Don't stop on my account," Jumbo groaned, tilting his head upward to watch the five women slathering his throbbing cock with their tongues.

"If you want some *more* of that stuff," Splashy said, forming a circle along with the other dwarves around the group of women. "There's five more of us, eager to share."

As each of the dwarves paired up with the women, they turned around and slurped their dicks bobbing excitedly in front of their faces.

"This one's cock is so much *bigger*," Clara said, humping her hips against the base of Jumbo's dick while she tightened her legs around his instrument.

"It's not only his *dick* that's huge," Clover nodded, rocking her hips against Jumbo's organ while she bounced atop his thick balls. "His *testicles* are almost as much fun to play with as his cock."

"But watch out for his *ejaculation*," Tara said. "If you're not careful, you'll be coated from head to foot with jizz."

"I like the sound of that," Sara said, humping her clit harder against Jumbo's shaft while she massaged the big dwarf's glans with the palms of her hands and simultaneously licked the underside of Splashy's crown.

"Oh God," Jumbo huffed, banging the back of his head against the floor while he curled his fingers into the shag rug lying underneath him. "I'm going to cum if you keep doing that–"

"You mean *this*?" Clover smiled, interlocking her fingers along with the other girls while they twisted their hands around the perimeter of his flaring glans and licked the heads of the other dwarves while they humped their hips in unison against the big dwarf's throbbing shaft.

"I mean *everything*," Jumbo grunted, peering up at Randy and Jessop who were standing over his head while Jessop rammed his hard-on into the other dwarf's cock-slit as they lashed their tongues together, watching the spectacle unfolding below them.

"Fuck, that's hot," Sara grunted, getting close to her own climax. "The men in our village have no idea what they're missing."

"I've seen some of them playing with each other behind the stables when no one is looking," Clara said. "I bet they'd love to try some of *these* pricks on for size sometime."

"If they knew how much fun these dwarfs were," her friend Tara nodded. "They wouldn't be so reluctant to have us steal away for a little distraction from time to time."

"I think I'd rather keep this secret between us girls," Sara shuddered, arching her back as she neared the tipping point.

"I'm going to come so hard," Clara nodded, knocking her knees against her friend while she humped Jumbo's thick organ.

"Me too," Tara said, interlocking her fingers with the other women as they squeezed Jumbo's flaring glans.

"Oh fuck," Jumbo hissed. "I can't hold it any longer. Here it comes, ready or not–"

Suddenly, the tip of his organ spewed a geyser of cream high into the air in a series of thick spurts, landing atop the heads of the five women while they squirmed around the base of his dick, shaking their asses and sucking the other dwarves as they came over their faces. When Jessop saw the five women squealing together in mutual climax, he grabbed the end of Randy's swelling organ and rammed his dick deep into his hole, grunting in ecstasy while the other dwarf spurted his syrup all over his quivering balls. By the time all of the dwarfs had emptied their loads in front of the women, the entire floor was coated in a thick puddle of cum.

But just as everyone was recovering from their powerful orgasms, a loud banging came from the front door of the cottage.

"Open up!" a man's voice bellowed from outside while Clover and her friends heard rustling coming from the other sides of the cottage.

"We know you've got our women," another man yelled from a nearby window, smashing it open with a large rock.

"It's time you paid for your sins," a third man said, flinging a Molotov cocktail into the cabin while a posse of townsmen circled the cottage, holding pitchforks and flaming arrows.

Clover and her friends leaped up, grabbing their weapons lying next to their discarded clothes.

"Something tells me your jealous boyfriends had some *other* form of entertainment in mind for our amorous dwarfs," she said. "I don't think they're so interested in sampling their wares as they are in eliminating their competition. You girls best be leaving while you still have a chance."

9

Within seconds, the mob had broken down the front door and swarmed inside the cabin, brandishing pitchforks and butchers' knives while they peered at the spectacle of the seven dwarfs with their still-tumescent organs dripping long strings of cum next to the three naked village girls. The girls quickly picked up their clothes lying on the floor and ran out the front door, terrified what the men would do when they saw them consorting with the well-endowed dwarfs. The leader of the band noticed Clover and her friends standing next to the dwarfs, holding their weapons in front of their exposed bodies.

"Who are you?" he said.

"We're friends of the dwarves," Tara said.

"Have you been participating in this debauchery also?" he snarled.

"We haven't done anything unlawful or harmful to your community," Clover nodded. "You've got your women back, now leave us in peace."

"I'm afraid it's not going to be that simple," the man said, slinging a heavy axe over his shoulder. "These freaks have been debasing our women for too long and producing mutant offspring that are polluting our gene pool. I'm afraid we're going to have to eliminate the source of this witchery, once and for all."

"Over our dead bodies," Jessop said, taking a step forward, swinging his saber in front of his chest.

"If that's the way you want it," the man said. "We'll be happy to oblige."

He nodded toward one of his associates, and the henchman lurched toward Jessop with an outstretched pitchfork. Moments later, Clover snapped the end of her bullwhip resting by her side, cracking a welt on the side of the man's forearm, and he yelped in pain, dropping the pitchfork onto the floor.

"We can do this the *easy* way or the hard way," she smiled, cracking the tip of her whip inches away from the ringleader's face.

"There's three of you and *twenty* of us," the man scoffed. "Six and a *half*, if you count the pigmy dwarfs. How do you expect to win against these odds?"

"We don't need the help of the dwarves," Tara said, placing the end of an arrow against her bowstring and drawing it firmly back, drawing a bead on the leader's chest. "They're lovers, not fighters."

"Two girls and a *boy*?" the leader scowled disdainfully, glancing at their glistening bodies coated with cum. "You've got to be kidding me."

"Test us, and find out for yourself," Clover said, flexing her legs in preparation for an attack.

The leader peered at her naked body, running his eyes

up and down her lithe figure, and licked his lips as one corner of his mouth tilted into a lopsided smile.

"It's a shame to defile such a lovely figure," he said. "But me and the rest of the men will enjoy having our way with you once we're finished killing the dwarfs."

He nodded toward the rest of the posse squeezing through the door, then he raised his ax over his head, flinging it end-over-end toward Jessop. Jessop ducked out of the way just in time as the rest of the group rushed toward the trio while the dwarves scurried for cover, throwing whatever household objects they could at the horde while the three friends weaved and bobbed among the melee, slowly dropping the attackers with their skillful use of weapons.

With an arrow deeply embedded in one of his shoulders, the ringleader picked up his fallen ax and swung it menacingly toward Clover while Randy threw the pot of steaming rabbit stew onto his back, making him scream in pain. Jessop quickly took advantage of the moment of vulnerability, driving his lance through the ringleader's abdomen, causing him to crumple to the floor while the rest of his dwindling crew hightailed it to the woods.

After everybody collected themselves and made sure the remaining attackers were no longer a threat, Clover peered over at the seven dwarfs, still cowering in fear behind the large sofa near the fireplace.

"Is everyone okay?" she said, helping them slowly to their feet. "Is anybody hurt?"

"Miraculously, no," Randy said, dusting off his naked body. "Thanks to your help. Where did you learn to fight like that?"

"We've been in a lot of scrapes along our journey," Tara

chuckled. "We've had a fair amount of practice fighting off hooligans like these along the way."

"Well, you saved our skins, and we're deeply indebted to you," Randy nodded.

"Unfortunately," Clover said, glancing out one of the broken windows and noticing a large plume of black smoke rising above their thatched roof. "I'm not sure we can say the same about your little cabin."

"Oh no!" Randy said, rushing outside with the rest of his friends to watch their home erupting in a giant fireball, sending tall flames above the surrounding treetops.

"What are we going to do *now*?" Noisy cried while their home slowly began to crumble into a pile of ashes. "We've got nowhere else to go."

"We'll just have to rebuild," Randy said, crossing his arms over his chest defiantly. "It shouldn't take too long if we all chip in together."

"We'll be happy to help," Clover said as she, Tara, and Jessop wrapped their arms around the tearful dwarves.

"There won't be any need for that," I woman's voice said from the edge of the woods as Sara and her friends and a collection of other young maidens from the village emerged from the side of the forest, walking toward the group and interlocking their arms around the group in a show of mutual support. "You're welcome to live with us in the village. You're much better lovers than our husbands anyhow."

"What about the rest of the men?" Randy said, noticing the girls' nightgowns clinging tightly to their bodies in the absence of their usual undergarments.

"The few that survived after you dispatched their mates ran off in fear for their lives. It appears that you can have us all to yourselves now."

"That's very kind of you," Randy said, turning toward his bandmates, who nodded excitely in agreement. "But what about making *babies*? Are you sure you won't mind a few more little dwarves popping up from time to time?"

"Not in the least," Clara smiled. "If they're as sweet and generous as *you* lot, I say good riddance to that abusive bunch of philanderers."

"Okay," Randy said, glancing around the collection of pretty women standing next to them. "But there's own seven of us and scores of you. How will we share the spoils amongst the entire group?"

"Don't worry about that," Sarah said, caressing his long dong hanging between his legs. "You've got more than enough manhood between the group of you to satisfy all of our needs. Would you care to join us and pick up where we left off?"

Randy paused for a moment while he turned toward Clover, Tara, and Jessop.

"What will you do now?" he said. "You're welcome to join us if you wish."

"I think you'll have your hands full with this group of sexy maidens," Clover chuckled. "Don't worry about us. We've always been restless wayfarers. We'll find another adventure around the next corner. Perhaps we'll meet you again on our return journey. You never know when we might need another dose of your secret sauce."

"We'll be waiting for you," Randy laughed, wrapping his arms around two of the women's shoulders and waving goodbye as he and his brethren trotted happily off toward the local village.

～

Ready for more erotic chills and thrills? Read the next exciting volume in Clover's Fantasy Adventures, *The Land of Mutants*. Buy direct and save at victoriarusherotica. Or download from your favorite online bookstore here: retailer links.

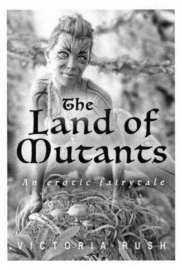

When it comes to sex organs, there's no such thing as having too many...

ALSO BY VICTORIA RUSH

Adult Fairytales:

The Enchanted Forest: An Erotic Fairytale

The Land of Giants: An Erotic Fairytale

The Dragon's Lair: An Erotic Fairytale

Witch's Brew: An Erotic Fairytale

The Mage's Spell: An Erotic Fairytale

The Mermaid Lagoon: An Erotic Fairytale

The Coven: An Erotic Fairytale

Rapunzel: An Erotic Fairytale

The Seven Dwarfs: An Erotic Fairytale

The Land of Mutants: An Erotic Fairytale

The Erotic Temple: A Sexy Fairytale (Coming Soon)

Erotica Themed Bundles:

Voyeur: Lesbian Erotica Bundle

Public Affairs: A Lesbian Anthology

Futa Fantasies: The Ladyboy Collection

Threesomes: The Lesbian Collection

Threesomes - Volume 2: The Lesbian Collection

First Time: A Lesbian Anthology

Hedonism: An Erotic Anthology

Switch Hitters: Bisexual Erotica

Taboo Erotica: The Lesbian Series

BDSM: The Lesbian Collection

Party Games: The Erotic Collection

Party Games 2: The Erotic Collection

All Girl 1: Lesbian Erotica Bundle

All Girl 2: Lesbian Erotica Bundle

All Girl 3: Lesbian Erotica Bundle

All Girl 4: Lesbian Erotica Bundle

Erotic Fairytale Bundles:

Clover's Fantasy Adventures: Books 1 - 5

Clover's Fantasy Adventures: Books 6 - 10

Erotic Fantasy:

Pirate's Bounty: A Time Travel Adventure

Wild West: A Time Travel Adventure

Private Riley: A Time Travel Adventure

Cleopatra's Secret: A Time Travel Adventure

Bounty Hunter 2125: A Time Travel Adventure

Ninja Assassin: A Time Travel Adventure

The 300: A Time Travel Adventure

Arabian Nights: An Erotic Fairytale (coming soon...)

Steamy Time Travel Bundles:

Riley's Time Travel Adventures: Books 1 - 5

Lesbian Erotica:

Tribadism 1: Girls Only Sex Workshop

Tribadism 2: The Art of Scissoring

Tribadism 3: Threeway Hookups

The Kiss: A Game of Oral Sex

Pledge Week: Sorority Sisters

Carny Games 1: A Wild Sex Party

Carny Games 2: A Kinky Sex Party

Carny Games 3: An Erotic Sex Party

Dreamscape: An Artificial Reality Game

Glory Hole: Guess Who's On the Other Side

Joy Ride: A Late Night Erotic Bus Trip

The Blind Girl: An Erotic Romance(Coming Soon)

Lesbian Erotica Bundles:

Jade's Erotic Adventures: Books 1 - 5

Jade's Erotic Adventures: Books 6 - 10

Jade's Erotic Adventures: Books 11 - 15

Jade's Erotic Adventures: Books 16 - 20

Jade's Erotic Adventures: Books 21 - 25

Jade's Erotic Adventures: Books 26 - 30

Standalone Stories:

The Polynesian Girl: A Lesbian EroticRomance

FOLLOW VICTORIA RUSH:

Want to keep informed of my latest erotic book releases? Sign up for my newsletter and receive a FREE bonus book:

Spying on the neighbors just got a lot more interesting...

Milton Keynes UK
Ingram Content Group UK Ltd.
UKHW042312240324
439966UK00004B/298